Pancake Dreams

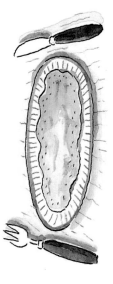

Ingmarie Ahvander
Pictures by Mati Lepp

Translated by Elisabeth Kallick Dyssegaard

R&S BOOKS

Stockholm   New York   London   Adelaide   Toronto

Stefan has a grandma called Elsa. She lives in Sweden, but Stefan now lives in Jordan, far away from there. It takes many hours to fly from Sweden to Jordan.

Before Stefan moved with his family, he and Grandma lived close to each other. Then they used to see each other a lot.

Grandma Elsa has always liked to cook. She always had something good to eat when Stefan and his brother came to visit: meatballs or homemade strawberry jam or Swedish pancakes. Stefan liked them all—most of all the pancakes. They were particularly delicious.

Sometimes he helped make them. Then they were specially made and extra good. He claimed that Grandma made her pancakes using only eggs and flour. Nothing more.

Stefan's mom wondered what kind of tooth-cracking pancakes they could be. Eggs and flour. Didn't that just make cement balls?

"No," said Stefan. "The pancakes are super good."

Stefan often thought of his grandma. He often thought of the pancakes.

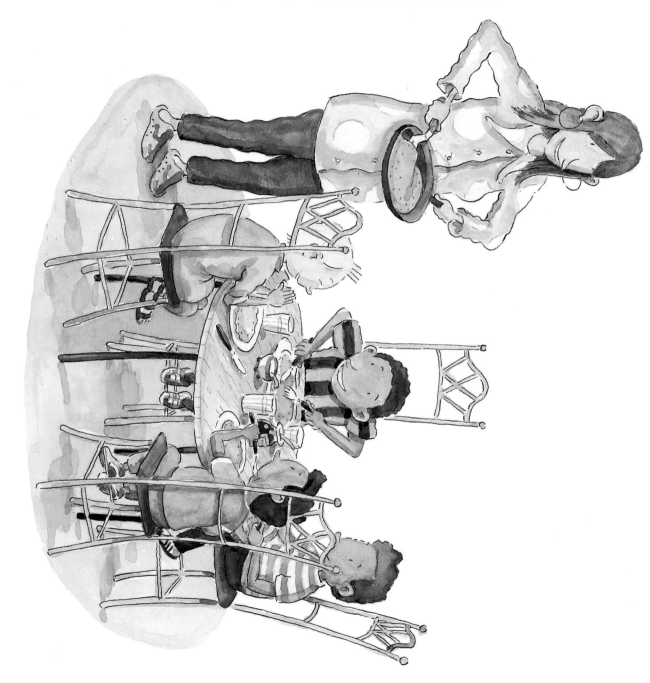

Mom made pancakes, too, but somehow it wasn't the same. They didn't taste the same.

Sometimes Mom made pancakes for Stefan and his friends. Ahmed, Mayank, and Deniz gobbled them up. Then Stefan would tell them about Grandma's pancakes.

"Specially made. Of flour and eggs," he would say.

One evening, when neither Mom nor Dad felt like cooking, they went to Muhammad's restaurant for dinner. On the way home they stopped to buy big, round, flat, freshly baked bread.

Since they bought a lot of bread, the baker put it in a box. It looked almost like a pizza box. Square. Good for bread. Good for pizza as well. But perhaps even better for pancakes . . .

Suddenly Stefan had an idea.

"Can't we mail this box to Grandma? Then she can bake pancakes and put them in the box and mail it back to me."

Both Mom and Dad thought that was a wonderful idea. The idea, that is. But, in reality, it would be hard to do, said Dad.

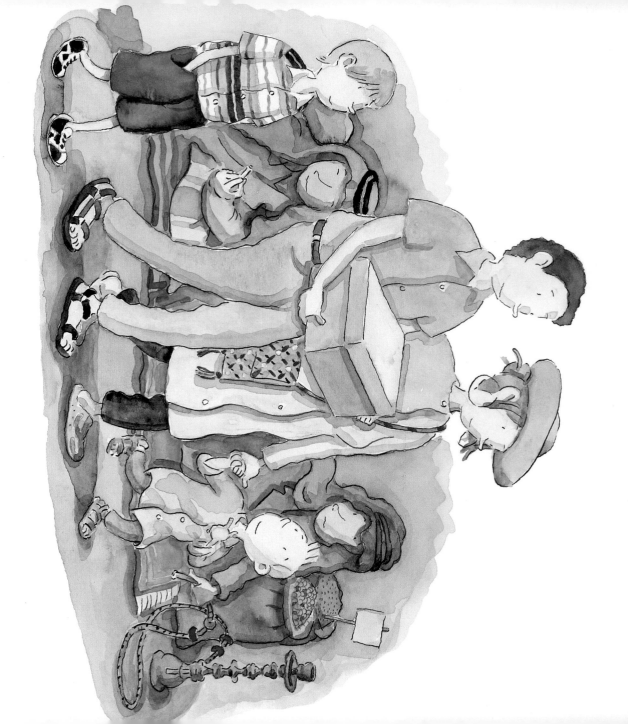

There were two problems. If the box was sent by mail, it might get smashed before it reached Grandma. Not a good container for pancakes. If the box made it to Grandma in one piece, how could it be mailed back? By the time it arrived, the pancakes would be all smashed into mush-cakes, not pancakes made from Grandma's special batter!

"If someone we know goes to Sweden, perhaps he or she can take the box to Grandma," Mom suggested.

When they got home and put the bread in a bag, Stefan put the box on a shelf in the pantry to wait for transportation to Sweden.

One day Aunt Martha showed up for an unexpected visit. She was an adventurous, determined, and sturdy woman and a friend of Grandma's. Aunt Martha was used to transporting odd things home. She was carrying lampshades, jingle bells, and jugs, so she had no problem taking a box as well.

When she got home, she delivered the box to Grandma. Inside was a note from Stefan.

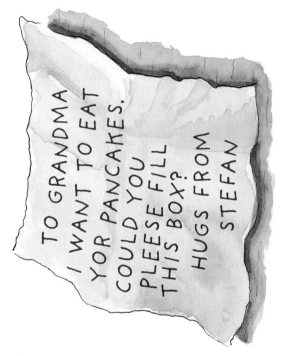

TO GRANDMA
I WANT TO EAT
YOR PANCAKES.
COULD YOU
PLEESE FILL
THIS BOX?
HUGS FROM
STEFAN

Grandma very much wanted to send pancakes to her grandson, but how could she? She couldn't put stamps on the box and mail it. The pancakes would get moldy before they arrived. Grandma had to find someone who was going to Jordan. Martha had already been there; she couldn't help. After a couple of days of thinking, Grandma put an ad in the paper:

Are you traveling to Jordan?
Responsible person sought for
pancake transportation. One box.
Tel. 0123-796 58 32

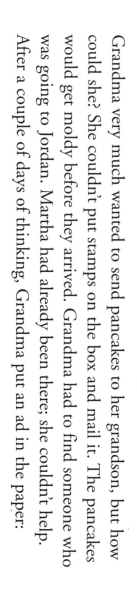

Several days passed, but then a man called to say that he was in fact going to Jordan.

"If it's just one box, I can take it. I have business to do in Amman. But please wrap the pancakes because I don't want them to stain my clothes. I assume I'll have to hold the box on my lap," said the man, whose name was Mr. Zetterkvist.

"Thank you very much," exclaimed Grandma happily, and she went right to work whipping up a pancake batter. She made pancakes for several hours. So they wouldn't stick together, she cut out pieces of wax paper to separate the layers.

Finally the box was so full that not even the smallest pancake could be added. Grandma made sure that the wax paper covered the pancakes properly so they wouldn't drip on Mr. Zetterkvist. Then she wrote a note, folded it, and taped it to the box.

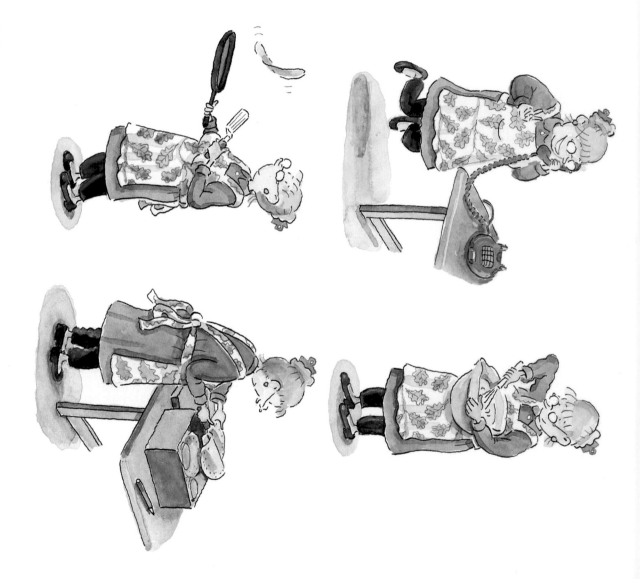

Early the next morning Grandma met Mr. Zetterkvist at the airport and gave him the box.

There was no problem in taking it on the airplane. Mr. Zetterkvist didn't need to hold it on his lap.

A flight attendant offered to put it on a shelf.

"But please don't crush it," Mr. Zetterkvist instructed.

On arrival in Amman, in Jordan, Mr. Zetterkvist had to go through customs before he could leave the airport. Everyone had to do that.

In customs you had to show that you were not bringing dangerous things into the country.

Mr. Zetterkvist balanced the box in one hand and walked toward the exit. A customs officer looked him over and nodded at the box.

Mr. Zetterkvist stopped and placed the box in front of the customs officer, who began to pull at the string to see what was in the box.

Then the customs officer sniffed curiously and lifted the lid.

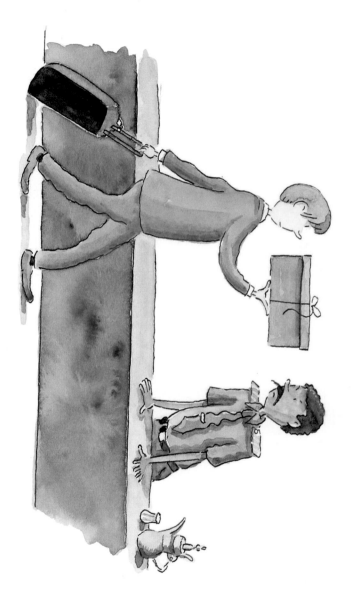

There lay the stacks of pancakes. The customs officer looked up at the man from Sweden and smacked his lips.

"Food? Good?" he asked in Arabic.

Mr. Zetterkvist nodded. The customs officer peeled loose a piece of pancake and popped it in his mouth. Then he chewed and smiled.

"*Taeeb!* It tastes very good," he observed and tore off another piece of the top pancake.

Now even Mr. Zetterkvist was tempted and couldn't help taking a piece as well. So the two men shared what was left of the top pancake.

But suddenly Mr. Zetterkvist put the lid back in place and explained in a little Arabic, a little English, and by making gestures that the pancakes were a present. They must not eat up the whole present.

The customs officer waved and nodded understandingly, and then Mr. Zetterkvist was allowed to go through to the main hall in the airport.

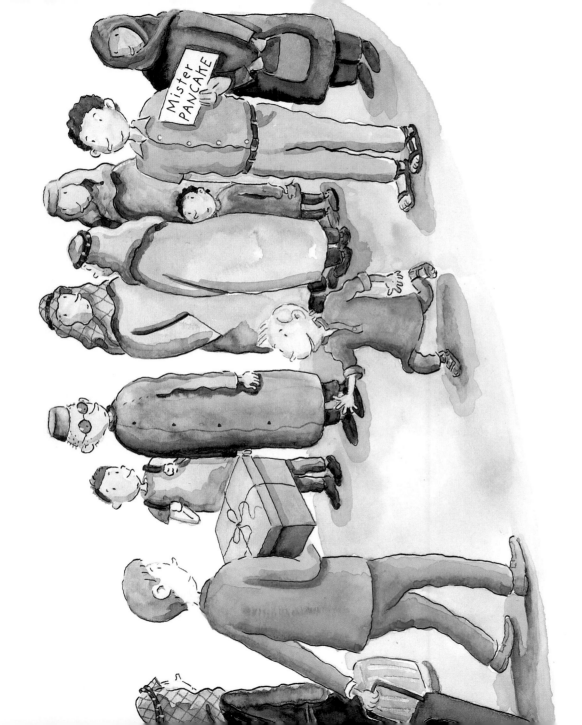

Stefan had been told which flight Mr. Zetterkvist was arriving on, so Dad and he were waiting. When Stefan saw a man holding a box, he ran toward him.

"Are you the man carrying Grandma's pancakes?" he asked expectantly.

"Yes, here they all are," said Mr. Zetterkvist and handed the box to Stefan.

Dad and Stefan thanked him for the transportation and Dad asked if Mr. Zetterkvist wanted a ride.

When they had taken Mr. Zetterkvist to his hotel, they headed home. Stefan sat in the car with the box on his knees, grinning. Soon he'd be eating super pancakes that Grandma had made just for him.

When they were finally home, Stefan carried the box with great ceremony up the stairs, into the hall, and directly to the dining room table.

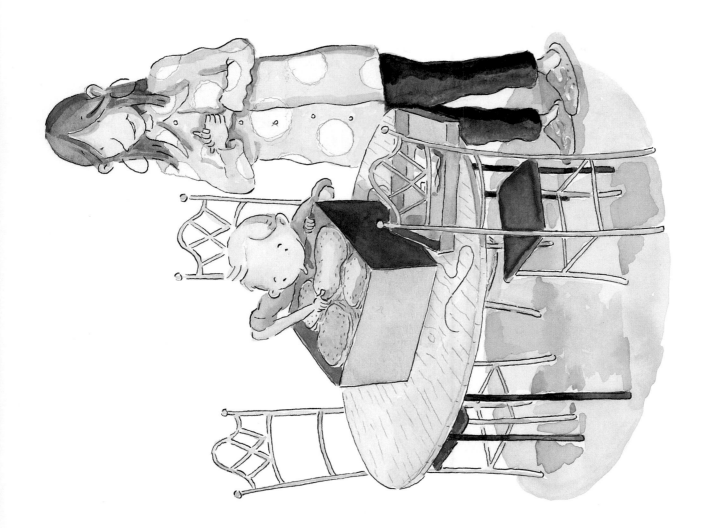

Mom suggested that they warm the pancakes in the oven, but Stefan didn't want to wait.

He took off the lid and had a first bite. It really tasted like Grandma's pancakes. He rolled up the rest of the pancake and stuffed it into his mouth. He chewed the whole pancake, and it felt wonderful.

He ate the next pancake with a little jam, and the next with butter and sugar, and the next one slid right down. So he kept going like that.

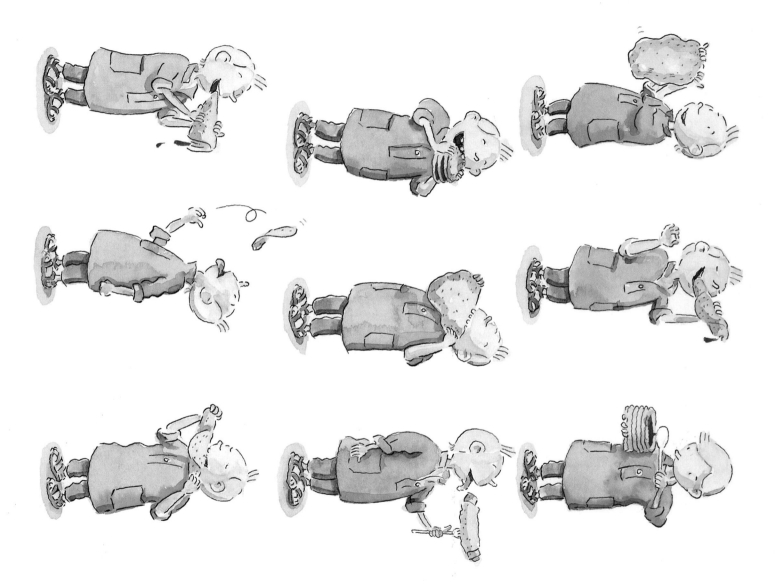

Mom, Dad, and Stefan's brother sat down at the table and looked longingly at him. Stefan's brother pressed his finger into the spilled sugar on the table and licked it off. A pancake crumb stuck to his finger and he licked it off right away.

When Stefan had eaten fourteen pancakes and the pile in the box had decreased considerably, he said that they could each have one pancake.

"But the rest are for me, and then Ahmed, Mayank, and Deniz get one each."
Stefan took a last pancake. It was a little bit hard to get it down, but it was so good. It was Grandma's . . .

*"Go ahead, eat as much as you like.
If the plate is empty, it'll be a nice day tomorrow!"*

That's what Grandma used to say when Stefan and his brother visited her.

The three pancakes for his friends were put on a plate and set aside.

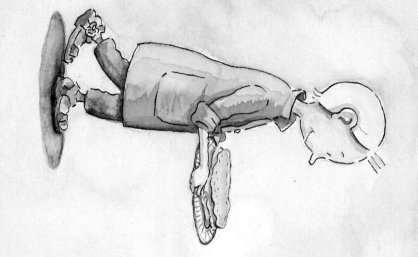

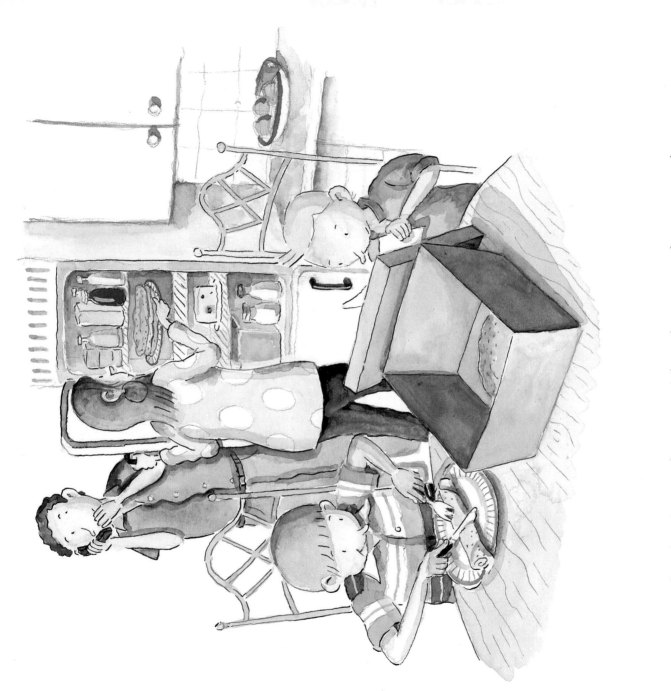

Stefan's brother ate four more. Then there was only one pancake left at the bottom of the box.

The note Grandma had taped to the box had come loose and stuck out. Stefan peeled it off the lid.

Stefan read it slowly and carefully. He thought of Grandma. Then he patted his stomach.

"I'll save the very last pancake for Grandma," he said and stretched out on the floor. "She's going to visit soon. I know it."

To my
pancake pal

Hugs from
Grandma

THE END

Rabén & Sjögren Bokförlag, Stockholm
http://www.raben.se

Originally published in Sweden by Rabén & Sjögren under the title *Farmors Pangkakor*
Text copyright © 2001 by Ingmarie Ahvander
Pictures copyright © 2001 by Mati Lepp
Library of Congress Control Number: 200109277
Printed in Denmark
First American edition, 2002
ISBN 91-29-65652-4

Rabén & Sjögren Bokförlag is a part of
P. A. Norstedt & Söner Publishing Group, established in 1823